John Ure

A Tour Round the World

John Ure

A Tour Round the World

ISBN/EAN: 9783337194055

Printed in Europe, USA, Canada, Australia, Japan

Cover: Foto ©Andreas Hilbeck / pixelio.de

More available books at **www.hansebooks.com**

A TOUR

ROUND THE WORLD.

BY AN

EX-LORD PROVOST

OF GLASGOW.

OUTWARDS—INDIA, AUSTRALIA.

PRINTED BY
ROBERT ANDERSON, 22 ANN STREET, GLASGOW.
1885.

IT will be seen that the following pages contain merely a record of impressions formed on a voyage round the world, a voyage made on the well-known beaten track. The places and incidents described are familiar to the ordinary traveller. The descriptions are mostly from memory unaided by notes; no profession is made of minute and exhaustive discussion. The Lecture is printed as it was delivered. It was delivered to audiences of different kinds; parts were selected to suit the different hearers; the sole excuse for printing at first was for convenience of selection of parts for delivery. That it now appears in its present form is due to the wish expressed by some friends, to read what they had not the opportunity of hearing.

JOHN URE.

CAIRNDHU,
BY HELENSBURGH, N.B.,
May, 1885.

A TOUR ROUND THE WORLD.

FTER seven-and-twenty years of continuous service in the Town Council, I felt that I had earned a rest, and I thought it best, when leaving the civic chair, to take my holiday then, and make a complete break between the work which hitherto I had been interested in and that with which I was henceforth to be engaged. Another reason I could give, if the whole truth must be told. I cherished the hope that, after a long absence, I might easily return to the city unnoticed and take my place quietly amongst my fellow-citizens. The first object of my leaving has been accomplished. I have had the relaxation, and a complete change of employment; but my appearance here this evening in this public capacity is an evidence that the fond hope of future privacy has altogether failed.

I had not long returned, when a polite note from the Secretary of the Athenæum informed me that the Directors of the Institution had in view a course of lectures for this winter; and that they were of opinion that a few words from me on the tour I had just completed, or on any part of it, would be very acceptable to the members. I replied to Mr. Lauder that I had not been anywhere that was not well known already. We followed the ordinary tourist route, which guide books and travellers' diaries made familiar to all; and

as I had not had the advantage which a predecessor
in office—Sir James Bain—had enjoyed of exploring
territory which no European had previously visited, I
could not add to the information already in possession of
the public ; and further, that not having contemplated
any such occasion as this, I had not been particular in
noting such incidents as would make a lecture either
interesting or instructive.   This answer did not satisfy
the Directors.   A deputation from them waited on me
at Helensburgh urging a reconsideration of my decision,
as they still believed the personal observations of one
so well known would be relished by my fellow-citizens.
At length I yielded to their solicitations, upon their
agreeing to accept all the responsibility of disappoint-
ment and failure.

When I began to think what I should say to you, I
soon came to the conclusion that if I was to convey an
intelligent idea of our whole journey, I must not be
particularly minute in description—that, to avoid undue
discursiveness, I must commit to writing what I meant
to say; and that I would more likely succeed in con-
veying correctly my impressions by using a plain con-
versational style than by making any attempt at fine
writing.   My paper, then, is mainly unadorned narrative.

Our party consisted of my wife and daughter, my
youngest son and myself, and I need hardly tell you
that such a journey as we contemplated required some
previous preparation.   There was the heat of India
to be encountered, and the cold of a New Zealand
winter to provide for ; there were long sea voyages
in our programme, and much land journeying by
road and rail.   The clothing suitable for all these

varied conditions had to be carried with us. Our heavy baggage, however, gave us little concern throughout the first stage of our journey, for we got our boxes on board the City of Cambridge, a 4,000-ton steamer, of Messrs. George Smith & Sons', at the Harbour of Glasgow, which carried us safely to Calcutta.

Our original intention, I may say, was to have travelled round the world, going westwards, and in certain seasons that is the right course to take; but when you cannot leave this country till the winter sets in, it is not proper to go by America, for in doing so you plunge into severe weather there, and would be crossing the Rocky Mountains when their snow covering is on. On the other hand, by taking the eastern route, starting at the time we did, you in three days step back, as it were, into summer, and may carry fine weather with you all the way round.

On 1st December, 1883, we joined the steamer at Liverpool, where she had proceeded from the Clyde to complete her loading. At noon we left the dock, sailed down the Mersey, and out to sea. In the afternoon we parted with the pilot off Holyhead, and proceeded onwards, passing the Scilly Isles next day, and were crossing the Bay of Biscay the two following days. Seamen laugh when landsmen speak with seriousness of special dangers in the Bay of Biscay, and certainly in my own experience there is nothing exceptional to be afraid of more than in any other part of the ocean. I have now crossed it three times, and always found comparatively smooth water.

On the early morning of the fourth day out we were abreast of Cape Finisterre, on the north-west coast of

Spain; from that day onwards all need of overcoats ceased—we had come to the genial temperature that permitted you to enjoy the fresh sea-breeze upon the steamer's deck, from which, as we coasted along past Spain and Portugal, we could, with a good glass, keep the land almost constantly in view.

At the end of the fifth day we passed the Straits of Gibraltar. All that afternoon we had been seeing a great number of both steam and sailing vessels making for or coming from the Straits. It is indeed the highway of nations—one of the gateways through which the Old and the New World travel when visiting each other. We passed Gibraltar at not more than two miles off the town and fortress. It was evening, and we could trace the streets and line of fortifications by the lights. It is one of our country's most valued strongholds, and from a careful inspection I had of it five years ago, I came to the conclusion that, so long as we desire to retain it, no enemy can ever wrest it from us. The Straits are nine miles wide, and quite within range of modern ordnance.

From thence to Malta was three days' sailing, and almost the entire distance in sight of the coast of Africa. The general impression I know is that Africa is a desert plain, but its appearance to us was quite the opposite of that. Along the southern shore of the Mediterranean, from the Straits of Gibraltar to Cape Bon, which is nearly a thousand miles, all the land you see is quite mountainous, and green foliage extends to the water's edge. On the eighth day we entered the harbour of Malta, that interesting dependency of the British Crown. The harbour is one of the finest in

the world, having an even depth of water throughout
sufficient for the largest ships to the very shore. Valetta,
the capital of the island is a fine city, containing many
large and beautiful public buildings; indeed, these seemed
much out of proportion to its importance as respects
either population or trade. It is essentially foreign in
its aspect; although belonging to Britain, comparatively
few of our own nation have settled there. French and
Spanish seemed to be the prevailing nationalities. The
value of Malta to Britain mainly consists in its capacious harbour, within which a fleet to command the
Mediterranean could safely ride under protection of
its fortifications, which are of enormous strength. We
had a view of St. Paul's Bay, where tradition says the
apostle was wrecked on his way to Rome. We spent
the day visiting other places of interest throughout the
island.

Before the sun went down we were again at sea, and
between Malta and the entrance to the Suez Canal
experienced the only really rough weather of the voyage. The second night after leaving Malta the wind
increased to what even a seaman would call "half a gale"—
the waves were running high, and at short intervals we had
the foredeck filled with water nearly up to the bul-
warks; our cabins were upon the upper deck, and
hitherto the ports could be kept quite open, but two of
my party neglected the precaution of shutting theirs on
this stormy night, and suffered accordingly, for a little
after midnight a heavy sea struck the vessel on the
starboard side, completely deluging their cabins, filling
their berths and thoroughly drenching themselves and
all their belongings. I was wakened by the loud noise,

and stepping into the adjoining cabin, I found the water surging about the floor at least six inches deep. The incident created some sensation amongst the passengers, who sympathised sincerely with the unfortunates, and cheerfully assisted the stewards in baling the water out. The untoward event was chronicled in the following verses, written by my daughter, who was one of the victims, entitled—

"THE RAID OF NEPTUNE."

The silence of night had fallen,
  And all but the sea was still ;
Weary folks dreaming sweetly,
  Or snoring with right good will.

But one eye still was waking,
  The eye of Neptune—the old
Neptune, the god of the ocean,
  Neptune the grim and the bold.

He rode on the top of the billows,
  And lashed his steed into foam ;
" As sure as my name is Neptune,
  Till morning I'll not go home.

" As free as the air of Heaven !
  Who can fetter the god of the sea ?
The winds and the waves have striven,
  They never can vanquish me ! "

One moment he paused in his fury,
  " Aha ! " he laughed in his glee,
" A port-hole, half-way open,
  There's room enough there for me."

With a howl and a yell most dreadful,
  With a swish and a splash and a roar,
He was in at that open port-hole,
  And lay rolling about on the floor.

His very eyes were sparkling
  With phosphorescent light,
As he seized my goods and chattels,
  And tossed them with all his might.

Still onward he rode in fury,
  And soon I felt upon me
The touch of his cold, icy fingers,
  I roared—but not in my glee.

Then out of my cabin he rushed,
  And down the saloon with a roar ;
Up started the sleepers in fright,
  They thought the ship was ashore.

He only smiled more grimly,
  And grinned at the havoc he made ;
" You may catch me now if you can,
  I am off on a midnight raid."

But great is the power of man,
  And the stewards were men every one ;
With buckets and pails they appear on the scene,
  And brave old Neptune is done.

Weird was that midnight scene
  In the cabin's dim flickering light,
As shivering forms were flitting—
  Best hid by the merciful night.

Some forms were dark in the twilight,
  In robes of dusky hue,
While some were white like linen,
  And, shuddering, looked so blue.

Then one by one these forms,
  The dusky and the white,
Crept back to their cabin's damp shelter,
  And again there was stillness and night.

By the following morning the sea had gone greatly
down, and continued moderate to the termination of our

Mediterranean voyage. We entered the Suez Canal at
Port Said, on the thirteenth day after leaving Liverpool.
On the following day we took our place in a procession
of steamers through that gigantic work of inland navigation. Its width for many miles appeared to be about
the same as the Clyde above the bridges, as it passes
Glasgow Green; but the banks were much higher,
indeed, it was only from the upper deck, and sometimes
only by ascending the rigging, that you could see to
the country beyond. I had the opportunity of witnessing the mirage as we sailed along. I was on
the bridge beside the captain, and remarked to him
that it was quite contrary to my expectation to see
the country so well watered. "Water?" he said, "that's
all desert you are looking on. There's not a drop of
water there." I could hardly believe it; but, as we
proceeded and the scene constantly changed, I became
convinced that it was wholly an optical illusion. What
appeared to be beautiful lakes, with fertile islands,
vanished like a dream as our position changed. Some
distance from Port Said we came to a ferry crossing
the canal. It was the highway from Cairo to Jerusalem.
A caravan, consisting of a score or more of camels, with
merchandise, was waiting at the ferry till the steamers
passed. The gay costume of the drivers brightened up
the bleak landscape, and gave a most picturesque appearance to a spot otherwise unattractive.

Now and again, as we sailed along, a solitary traveller
might be observed on the sandy waste on camel's back;
but, so far as I can recollect, we saw no village on the
route, but only at the stations where vessels draw into
the side to allow others to pass were there a few houses

to accommodate those working the canal. The first night we anchored in the small lake in front of Ismalia, where we all landed, and on donkeys rode up through the town. The next day we proceeded onwards in the same order of procession—it being a fixed regulation that no vessel shall pass another which is before it excepting while sailing through the Bitter Lake, which is about eight miles in extent.

We were in hopes of reaching Suez the second night, but a detention at the Bitter Lake kept us back, and so we had to anchor in the Canal seven miles from its termination, and, as it happened, exactly opposite one of the battlefields of a few months before. It was bright moonlight; nearly all our passengers landed and walked over the scene of conflict, bringing back trophies to the ship. By ten o'clock the following day we were through, and cast anchor in front of the little town of Suez.

It is an old saying, "that there is nothing new under the sun," and probably in no part of the world are we more likely to find old things in view than in the land of Egypt.

This present Suez Canal, which forms the connecting link betwixt the Mediterranean and the Red Sea, will take rank in history as one of the great engineering works of the nineteenth century; and yet it has to be admitted that it is only the resuscitation of an old canal which was made by the Egyptian Kings many hundreds of years ago, and it is even doubtful if the Ptolemy who gets credit for the conception of it was really the first constructor, for there are two separate periods, many years distant in time from each other, that a canal is known

to have existed betwixt the Mediterranean and the Red
Sea—the presumption being that the shifting sands of the
desert had in the interval filled the first up, as it also
did the second. Of course neither of these canals were
suitable for the passage of such large vessels as now use
the navigation. Towards the end of last century the
first Napoleon Bonaparte proposed the remaking of the
old canal. And quite likely it would have been commenced in his time but for a mistake made by his
surveying engineer, who reported that the Red Sea
level was 33 feet higher than the waters of the Mediterranean. British engineers, however, subsequently dis-
covered that the difference in level is only six inches; but
they thought it quite impracticable, believing that the drift-
ing sand of the desert was sure to fill it up, as it had
done before; and, indeed, that is found to be very nearly
the case—dredging operations on an extensive scale are
required continually, and is a never-ending cause of
anxiety and expense. There happened to be very little
wind blowing when we passed through, but I was
informed that vessels were sometimes so deluged with
sand that it has to be shovelled off their decks in ton
loads. The length of the canal is about 99 miles, and
the constructed breadth just about what I have already
mentioned, but nearly one-third of its course is much
wider, that is where it passes through natural lakes or
water holes. The depth for navigation is understood
to be not less than 26 feet, even at the shallowest
part.

The sail in the Canal was novel and interesting,
enlivened, as it had been, by the passage of a large
number of steamers. In the two days we were in it we

met upwards of twenty, not one of them under 3,000 tons burthen, and I am proud to say that, with the exception of one French War Frigate and one Russian Man-of-War, all the vessels we saw were flying the British flag.

On leaving the Canal you enter the Gulf of Suez, an arm of the Red Sea, which is quite narrow at first, but widens out as you proceed, until it is so broad that you are frequently out of sight of land altogether. What land we did see was mountainous. Mount Sinai was pointed out to us, distant about seventy miles. The atmosphere was so clear, however, as to make it appear not half that distance away.

At some seasons it is a great trial to pass down the Red Sea because of the heat. We were favoured with a good breeze, and it being winter the temperature was delightful, never more than seventy-nine degrees in the shade; the water was warmer than the air, for it was not under eighty-two degrees, consequently it was very pleasant to bathe in. The baths in the steamer were much in use during the voyage.

We pass out of the Red Sea through the Straits of Bab-el-Mandeb, known as "The Gate of Tears," so named from the numerous wrecks that in former times occurred upon this desolate coast. There is now a British lighthouse there on the Island of Perim. How that solitary Island came into our possession I have heard related thus:—When the Suez Canal, which you may remember was at first entirely a French undertaking, approached completion, the French Government foresaw that this route to India was to assume an importance which had not previously attached to it, and that a fortress on the Island of Perim at the Straits would command the Red Sea as effectually as Gibraltar does the Mediterranean, and so they sent two war ships out to take possession of the Island for France. They had to go by the Cape, as the Canal was not yet open. These vessels called at Aden, a British coaling station on the Arabian coast, on their way to the Straits. The Governor politely invited the French officers to dine with him. Over their wine it came out what the object of their visit to Perim was. The Governor, without rising from the table, pencilled a note to the commander of a British gunboat then lying in the harbour to get up steam at once and proceed to the Island of Perim and take possession of it for Her Majesty. The order was at once obeyed, and when the two French war ships got to Perim they found it in the hands of the British, whose flag was now waving over it. I cannot tell whether the Governor was raised to the peerage for his prompt and timely action, but I am sure you will agree with me that some who have sat in the House of Lords had that honour conferred on them for less meritorious services.

After passing out of the Red Sea, for three days we were in sight of the east coast of Africa, and on the other side got glimpses of Arabia. The next land we saw was the Island of Socotra at a great distance. It lies 140 miles off Cape Guardifui—the furthest east point of Africa,—and is inhabited by a wild Beduin race, who make slaves of any unfortunate shipwrecked mariners who may chance to fall into their hands; and we were informed that the Governor of Aden had authority to give a ransom of five pounds a head for any British subjects they might bring to him, which sum they would lose if he required to send to the island for them. Six days thereafter we came in sight of the lovely Island of Ceylon, on the south of India. We coasted along an entire day, and had the pleasure of looking upon its luxurious vegetation, which reached down to the golden strand. We could see the tall cocoa-nut palm trees with their graceful leaves springing from the top; and mountains, as far as the eye could reach, covered with trees or rich verdure. We knew that we had to return to Ceylon to join the Australian Mail Steamer, and this passing glimpse created a strong desire to see more of this lovely land. Four days sailing brought us to the mouths of the Ganges. On nearing the Hooghly, and long before you enter it, you are sensible that you are approaching a great river by the changed colour of the water. Hitherto we had been ploughing our way through the bright blue ocean; now the waves, although still the mighty waves of the sea, are without doubt the discoloured waters of the Ganges. The banks of the river are very flat; in fact, you have proceeded some miles up before being sensible that the black streak which you see on either side a mile or more distant is really land, and it is only after you have sailed for some hours in the smooth but turbid waters, and are meeting many native boats with swarthy boatmen, that you feel sure you are now within the realm of Queen Victoria, the Empress of India.

It takes a whole day's steaming from the entrance of the river till you reach Calcutta; but as you proceed

the stir upon the river increases; the scenery improves,
giving place to cultivated fields, with here and there
a native village ; as you get nearer to the great
city, there are to be seen the handsome residences of
Calcutta merchants, and the splendid palace of at least
one native Prince.   It was evening before we cast
anchor at Garden Reach, immediately below the
crowded harbour, which no vessel is allowed to enter
after sundown.   The following morning we landed at
Calcutta.   The city, as seen from the steamer's deck,
is very imposing.   In front of you stands Government
House, with its handsome gateway facing the river ;
to the right a range of large palatial buildings, with
pillars in front, the residences of the European gentry.
At the extreme end, and a little removed from them, is
the new Cathedral; and but a short distance off the
extensive Law Courts.   Again, separated from these
buildings by a wide plain, stands Fort-William, one of
the largest fortresses in India, but presenting nothing
very striking in general appearance.   Our steamer was
still at anchor in the river, as the berth she was to
occupy was not yet vacant, and so we had to land in
a small boat, which brought us to the jetty, beside
which large numbers of natives of both sexes were
disporting themselves in the water, crowds of them
going out and in continually.   It was a lively scene,
and such as we had never previously witnessed.   The
Great Exhibition was now opened, and hotels and
boarding-houses were all full; but we had secured rooms
in the Great Eastern Hotel, preferring to go there
rather than accept the kind hospitality pressed upon us
by those to whom we were only known through letters

of introduction. We had to engage an Indian servant—those attached to the hotel are not expected to give visitors much attention—and, as there are no bells connected with the rooms, it would have been necessary to go to the clerk in the office for any requirement, except at public meals. But even at these, nearly every one has his private servant to attend to him, and where there is a party of four, one special attendant, at least, is indispensable. We had the assistance of a friend who was staying in the hotel in making a choice, and we were extremely fortunate, for the man we got was very capable, spoke our language fairly well, was most attentive, and studied our interests and comfort in every way. The only fault I had to find with Jeulim was that he persisted in doing for you all manner of things that a European, before he goes to India, is accustomed to do for himself; but Europeans very soon fall into lazy habits and let their servants perform every part of their toilet for them. As an interpreter between us and the natives he was invaluable; in protecting us from the persistent attentions of itinerant merchants on the streets and exorbitant charges in the shops he saved us his wages a hundred fold. In fact, we could not have done without him, and when giving him a testimonial at the termination of his month's service, I promised to write beforehand when we returned to India, and he engaged to travel across to Bombay and meet us there.

Our first outing was to the Exhibition. The Indian and foreign sections were very interesting to us; more curious than instructive, for the Eastern nations are far behind in all useful arts and manufactures. Carving ivory and metal, weaving cloth of gold and

embroidery, and such handicrafts they excel in. Labour-
saving machinery they know nothing of. We saw the
most primitive implements shown at the Exhibition as
the best of their kind. Where labourers can be had
for sixpence a day there is not the same inducement
as with us to lessen the number employed by the application of machinery. We saw at the Exhibition many
of the native Princes and inhabitants of distant parts
of India, the latter brought there at the expense of the
Government as a matter of education. On one occasion
when out walking I met a marriage procession on the
street. Marriages in India are celebrated at a very
early age, and always with extravagant expense. We
were told that in numerous instances the poorer Hindoos
ruin themselves by the outlay which thus following an
absurd custom entails. Our attention was attracted by
distant music, and as it approached we could observe,
following the pipers and drummers, a gaudy cavalcade
of horses with gay trappings, four of them harnessed to
a kind of raised platform, on which was seated, on a
mimic throne, in tinsel dress, the young bridegroom,
a child of 14 or so. He was being conveyed to his
young bride, and, along with his near relatives, who
surrounded the chariot on which he sat, greeted the
passers by serenely. The procession was a long one,
and entirely blocked the streets it passed along.

Several times we returned to the Exhibition, more with
a view to study the native character than to examine
their productions. From what I did see of the latter, however, I have no doubt of there being a great future for
India in providing wheat and wine for Western Europe.
The Indian wheat which I had seen in this country was

always inferior to other importations; but I was sure, from the bread that was laid on the hotel table, that the best sorts had not been sent home. The splendid variety shown at the Exhibition clearly demonstrated that. Through the kind attention of Dr. Watt, who had charge of the products section, I had every opportunity of examining it, and also of tasting the Indian wine, which, in my judgment, was excellent.

Of course we saw the places of interest which tourists usually visit in and around the city; but all these have been described so frequently that I think it unnecessary to occupy time in repeating what to many must be quite familiar. Calcutta I have heard called the "City of Palaces;" to call it the "City of Hovels" would be as truly descriptive. No doubt there are many fine buildings, quite palatial in their character, but the great mass of its teeming population are very poorly housed. We have nothing so wretched in this country in any of our towns; but then, the conditions are entirely different. Here, we need protection from the inclemency of the weather; there they only need a covering in the rainy season and from the rays of the sun; indeed, the scanty clothing which the natives wear—only a bit of calico round their middle—even in winter, shows the great difference from what our poor have to endure. The general cleansing of the city is not well performed. But since we were there a Public Health Society has been inaugurated under the Presidency of His Honour the Lieutenant-Governor of Bengal, and no doubt many improvements will result. Much of the heavy traffic of the streets is carried on bullock waggons, and the droppings from the cattle when dried makes cheap fuel for the natives. During day time no household fires are required, but when the morning and evening meals are preparing the smell of the smoke is sometimes overpowering. I never saw a scavenger at work all the time we were there, but during the stillness of the night we heard the yelping and howling of jackals as they prowled about, picking up garbage everywhere. One day, when out driving in an open carriage, I told our Indian servant that I wanted to go to the Salt Lakes, where the refuse from ashpits, &c., was deposited, and the sewage of the city drained to. The driver had never been there, and no stranger he said ever went to the place. As a sanitary reformer, however, it was in my line, and I wished to see it. After much inquiry, we found the direction; but, on nearing the outfall, we were driven back by the intolerable stench, the myriads of large flies, and the crowds of vultures hovering close over us.

Another place I visited which is not very attractive to sensitive natures—the Nimtollah Ghaut, where the dead are burned. I am not going to discuss the question here, although, as a sanitary reformer, I must admit that, on the side of the public health, cremation has the best of it; and certainly, as opposed to the practice which at one time prevailed, of throwing the dead into the river, the method now adopted is far preferable. The Burning Ghauts are on the river-banks within the city, but not near any other building. A high wall, entirely open above, surrounds a space of about 60 yards by 20. Within this enclosure several hollows like shallow graves are formed; across these openings billets of wood are placed, and the body is laid thereon; more wood is put over it, and the pile is set fire to—in two or three hours the work is done. It was four in the afternoon when I was there; two bodies were being consumed, both had died that forenoon. On the previous day the remains of the great Brahma leader, Baboo Keshub Chunder Sen, had been cremated there. The Indian in charge of the Ghaut, on being questioned through my interpreter respecting the ceremony, pointed to the small quantity of ashes left, saying, fifteen bundles of sandal-wood had been burned. He had never known more than twelve before. We could get nothing more out of him than that. In this man's estimation, Chunder Sen, the founder of a new faith not far from Christianity, was of more importance than his countrymen only to the extent of three bundles of sweet-scented sandal-wood.

It was the middle of winter, and the weather was most enjoyable when we first arrived; but it got gradually hotter, and one of my party feeling it more than the rest of us, we went inland about 360 miles to Darjeeling, amongst the wonderful mountain scenery of the Himalayas, and there, when the sun went down, we had it cold enough—indeed, so much so that it was necessary to keep fires on in our bedrooms throughout the entire night. The reason of the lower temperature there was its altitude above sea level, 7,500 feet, nearly twice the height of the highest mountain in Scotland; but even the great height of Darjeeling was as nothing compared to the snow-clad range that was in front of us. I shall never forget its appearance, and the conversation I had with our hotel-keeper the day we arrived. He said to me that, unless I meant to stay some time, I might not at that season get so favourable a day for having the different mountains pointed out, and so we

went with him to the verandah. He asked me if I
could guess the distance which the highest mountains we
were looking at were from us. I said I was familiar
with high hills in front of my residence at home, four
miles of water and two miles behind Greenock—six in
all. The mountains before us we could see more distinctly than I had ever seen the hills beyond Greenock;
but then I had never looked at them in so pure an
atmosphere, and I thought I was making a fair allowance when I named twelve miles. "Ah!" he said, "you
are far under it, for even the nearest range you see"
(which I had not before observed, as my attention was
taken up with the highest) "is fully twelve miles distant,
and the valley between us and it descends 5,000 feet from
where we stand; and those great peaks which appear so
near, and the fissures and chasms of which you see so
distinctly, are forty miles away,—their height is twenty-
eight and twenty-nine thousand feet." Never in this
world have I seen so sublime a spectacle. We had
looked on magnificent palaces and gorgeous temples,
but this was a temple not made with hands, before which
we were awe-struck, its stupendous heights reaching not
into the clouds, for there were none, but into the azure
blue with which the bright, clear, everlasting snow that
covered them formed a splendid contrast. *Himalaya*, in
Sanscrit, signifies "the abode of snow." We saw the
snowy range on subsequent days in varying conditions,
but never so beautiful as on the day of our arrival.

The journey to Darjeeling is a whole day's travelling.
We left Calcutta by rail at three in the afternoon, and
got to the station where we crossed the Ganges at eight;
dined on board the steamer while she was sailing up the

stream to another railway, where we got into sleeping-carriages; and, travelling all night, reached Silligouri,, at the foot of the mountains, just as the sun was rising, and, after breakfasting, started on the narrow gauge railway, only two feet wide, by which we arrived at Darjeeling about four in the afternoon. The gradient on the North British Railway from Queen Street Station to Cowlairs is 1 in 45, and the locomotive requires the aid of a cable wrought by two powerful engines in pulling the train up the incline. This mountain railway has an average gradient of 1 in 22 on thirty miles of its course, and would never have been made had not the Indian Government allowed the company who formed it to use the public highway wherever they could in climbing the mountains. In travelling up you can often look out of the carriages over precipices that you pass the edge of and look down more than 1,000 feet straight below. Darjeeling is situate on a projecting spur of Mount Senchul—the ground rapidly falling, on every side but one, to a depth of 5,000 feet in the valley below—which can only be reached by narrow bridal paths terraced on the mountain side. It is a small town of not more than a thousand inhabitants, but there is a Government Cantonment for 250 invalid soldiers, and a Sanitarium for 100 civilians.

Tea cultivation is the only industry, and the quality raised here bears a high character. Along with my daughter I rode down to a tea plantation on the mountain side, three thousand feet below, to visit a tea planter, to whom we had an introduction from a friend at Calcutta. We found him at his bungalo, and had the finest cup of tea I think I ever drank.

The natives here are a different race entirely from the slender Hindoo of the plains. The cast of countenance is quite changed. Amongst the Hindoos, many are really beautiful; but now we are amongst a people whose features are of a distinctly Mongolian type— broad, flat faces, eyes oblique, and high cheek bones; a sturdy race, looking capable of holding their own with any one. Even the women have a masculine look, and we were informed bear burdens that only strong men would be expected to carry elsewhere. An example of that was related to us as having occurred in the case of a lady who had a piano sent to her from Calcutta. She left her house on the hill-side to proceed to the railway station, a mile or more distant, to make arrangements for having it conveyed home, but, to her astonishment, she met the woman who did the rough work of the house struggling to get in at the narrow entrance gate with the instrument upon her back. The women are very industrious too. I don't recollect of ever seeing any idle, for if they were not working or carrying a burden of some kind they were sure to be whirling an ingenious spinning machine that was in every female's hand. From the verandah of our hotel we looked down on the market place of Darjeeling, four or five hundred feet below, and from thence, on Sunday, which was the principal market day, a sound arose from the mingling voices as of fifty dog kennels broken loose and mixed with the roar of breakers on the beach. On the same plateau as the market place stood the Buddhist Temple, a tawdry wooden building, decorated with gilding and gaudy colours, surrounded by a wall ten or twelve feet high, having a wide gate at the one end and a narrow door at the other. I sought entrance one day at the large gate, and whilst I stood a native policeman, who could speak some English, told me I could only get in at the little one. This was kept for Buddha's days. I went there and was admitted by the priests, who could not speak to me, but let me plainly understand that a rupee would buy me many prayers, and so, for that coin, the praying wheel that was within the temple was set a-going. It was a cylinder, like a drum, standing on an axle on end, and turned with a handle; round it, on paper slips, are written innumerable prayers, and the idea is, that each time the cylinder turns all these prayers are offered to the Deity within the temple. What a degradation of the human intellect is here— the turning of a wheel propitiating a Deity!

The rainy season was now imminent, and so we only stayed about a week at Darjeeling, and when we returned to Calcutta the heat was greater than before, so we had to give up our intention of crossing India to Bombay. The journey occupies six days of continuous travel, and the heat and dust would have made it fatiguing and uncomfortable.

Kind friends in Glasgow had given me letters to friends and correspondents in Calcutta; some of these I presented, but the result of making myself known was endless offers of hospitalities all the time we were there. The Anglo-Indian does his entertaining on a grand scale, and generally he has all the conveniences for doing so ready to his hand. His house is large, the apartments numerous, lofty, and capacious; he keeps a

retinue of servants that only a grandee or nobleman here
would have. One Calcutta merchant with whom we dined
informed me that he had thirty male and two female
servants. The two females attended to his wife and
daughter—the men servants did all the work. One
cannot at first realise the necessity for this great army
of domestics. It all arises from caste prejudices. Each
individual servant confines himself within a very narrow
sphere; he will only do one particular kind of work, and
you must have others to do that which he will not.
The man who dusts the furniture will not sweep the
floor, the man who sweeps the floor will not black your
shoes, the man who tidies your bed-room will not
remove the slops; if you keep a carriage the coachman
attends to it, but each horse must have its own attendant, called a Cice. You are thus in a manner
compelled to keep up a large body of servants.
Our friend kept six horses and two carriages; that
involved the services of twelve men about the stable—
six to take charge of the horses, other two as coachmen, two as grass-cutters, and two as water-carriers.
So far as I could observe, the employment of females in
domestic service was very limited, and generally in the
capacity of nursery maids, called Ayahs. I did, however,
see many of the lowest class of females working in the
jute mills. That department of work, for instance, which
is almost always performed by women with us—namely,
washing and dressing—is entirely in the hands of the
opposite sex in India; the Dhobie does all that, and
the finer descriptions of that work, such as washing and
dressing lace, is done by the Pinwallah. But indeed
throughout the colonies and in America much of the

work of the laundry is now performed by men, in
the latter country almost always by Chinese.

Amongst those who received us with great kindness
was the Viceroy, Lord Ripon, to whom I had creden-
tials from Lord Hartington. During our short stay we
had three invitations to Government House—to dine,
to an assembly, and to a levee. I had also the honour
of an interview with his Excellency.

To one who had fled from home to escape from the
numerous engagements of city life, this life in Calcutta
was no change at all, and so I determined to be
sparing with my introductory letters in future, although
perhaps, in doing so, I have disappointed friends here,
and may have offended some abroad. Four weeks after
our arrival we took our departure from Calcutta. I
could not help having a strange feeling of sadness as
I left it. The Ilbert Bill was the subject uppermost
in the minds of our countrymen there. Many of them
had dismal forebodings of its effect if passed into law.
They pointed to the handful of Europeans amongst the
millions of India. They firmly believed that if ever
those teeming masses came to think themselves capable
of self-government, which principle that bill was mainly
founded on, then the days of our rule in India were
numbered. I offer no opinion—indeed I have none
to offer—so limited an experience as mine would
not warrant me. I have seen those teeming masses—
wherever we went the population was immense—you
seemed never to lose sight of human beings even far
away from towns. Those inhabiting the plains appeared
to be a gentle, peaceful people, intent on serving you.
The inhabitants of the mountainous region were more

D

self-reliant and determined—from them generally our
troubles have come. It is fortunate for us that there
is no cohesion amongst the different castes in India,
and that they are more prone to be at enmity with
each other than with us ; but probably it is more
fortunate still that we can point to our rule over them,
in recent years at least, as having been entirely for
their good.

We had taken passages in the Peninsular and Oriental
Steamer for Colombo, and embarked at daybreak on
board the s.s. "Teheran." The sail down the Hoogly
is most interesting, not less on account of the native
villages on its banks, and here and there the handsome
residences of Calcutta merchant princes, as from the
innumerable native craft of every size and description
that you meet on the river, from the tiny canoe paddled
by a single native to the clumsy barge with sweeping
oars worked by a score or more of nearly naked
boatmen, bringing produce from the interior to the
great emporium, Calcutta. By the afternoon we had
parted with the pilot, and were once more at sea. The
voyage of three days across the Bay of Bengal to
Madras was uneventful ; the sea was as smooth as we
ever have it on the Firth of Clyde, and nothing
occurred to break the monotony of the voyage but an
evening concert, and the usual deck games that passengers indulge in who do not care to read or write.

At Madras we had the opportunity of going on shore
in the native surf-boats, propelled by eight rowers. An
ordinary ship's boat is no use for landing there ; it
would be knocked to pieces on the shore by the great
waves that continually roll in.

The surf-boat is as elastic as a wicker basket. No nails are used to fasten the planks—they are sewed together, and kept tight with pitch and cocoa-nut fibre. Immediately on touching the beach the men leap out and pull the boat in. You are then lifted out and carried to the shore. The natives have another kind of boat, or rather raft, which we only saw there and at Colombo. It is called a catamaran, and consists of three pieces of wood, about 10 feet long, tied together. The Indian squats on that, and the sea is constantly breaking over it. He propels himself with a piece of flat wood, and, we were told, ventured out in very stormy weather. One man came alongside the steamer in one of these rude contrivances, freighted with two large baskets of eggs.

Many of the natives came on board to sell small merchandise of various kinds, trinkets and curious puzzles. There were also the famous jugglers, of whom we had heard wonderful accounts. We saw the basket trick performed upon the quarter-deck. A middle-sized swarthy woman had her arms and ankles tied. She sat down upon a small flat basket, with a narrow opening into which it appeared impossible for her to get. The juggler held a black cloth covering her for a very few minutes, all the while whistling with a small pipe as if making an incantation. On removing the cloth the woman had disappeared, and the man, to show that she was not in the basket, pierced it at various places with a sword. Afterwards covering the basket, and on again removing the cloth she was found sitting over it and bound as before. Another trick that created much interest was putting a few handfuls of sand on the deck, planting a seed in it, covering it with a cloth, piping over it as in the basket trick, and in a little while lifting the cloth and finding a shrub six or eight inches high growing out of the sand. Other performances with live snakes were quite as startling, but by no means so pleasing to behold.

Madras may be said to consist of two towns quite distinct from one another. The White, inhabited by Europeans, the Black, by the native population. Looking from the steamer's deck there were in view many large and handsome buildings; but the principal business street, in which was the Post Office, was very narrow, and the houses small. We observed, as we passed through it, that on many of the door-posts and lintels were curious carvings of the real eastern pattern. The city generally, however, struck me as having an appearance of gloom about it, which suggested the idea that it had seen better days. I have since learned that an epidemic of smallpox was prevailing; and when I turn up the Registrar-General's reports I find that in the first three months of last year (and we were there in the middle of that time) upwards of 1,500 deaths had occurred in Madras from smallpox, and that the total mortality from all causes for the quarter had been at the rate of 70 per 1,000 per annum. You will have some idea of the calamity which such a death-rate involves, when I tell you that if the same death-rate had prevailed in Glasgow during the quarter, there would have been 5,698 more deaths in our city in the first three months of 1884 than actually occurred.

From Madras we next sailed to Colombo, which we reached just one week after leaving Calcutta.

Colombo has one of the finest breakwaters that I have
ever seen, constructed from designs by Mr. Kyle, of our
own city, who superintended its erection. The method
of construction is quite novel. The material used is
great blocks made of stones and cement, about twenty
feet by eight, weighing twelve to fifteen tons each, and
laid not flat on each other, but angled so that each
block gets a rest on more than one below it. The
breakwater at Madras was constructed in the usual
manner, at the same time as the one at Colombo, but
a great storm which swept over both two years ago
made great breaches at Madras but did no damage to
the one at Colombo. You may recollect that Arabi
Pasha has taken up his residence there. I repeatedly
passed the villa he resides in, and was always asked
by the driver if I was not going to call—who at the same
time informed me that many of my countrymen did who
came to Colombo with the steamers passing to or from
the East and the Colonies. I could not, however, regard
the man as a hero in any sense, neither could I forget
the blood and treasure he had cost my country and his
own. Although I might have a little curiosity, common
decency would have demanded a show of respect which
I really did not feel, and so I thought I had better stay
away. My daughter saw him at an assembly which
took place during our short stay, and she informed me
that the great Arabi and his suite partook of the evening's refreshment by themselves apart, using neither
spoons nor forks, but in true Eastern fashion helping
themselves to the dainties with their fingers. There
was, however, one eminent personage at Colombo while
we were there that I would have had great pleasure in

making my obeisance to. He came by the mail steamer
from Australia, and during her short stay went up to the
mountainous district of Ceylon by railway, returning just
in time to proceed homewards. It was only after the
steamer had sailed I learned that amongst her passengers,
returning from the Colonies, was the Right Hon. the
Earl of Rosebery. Colombo is now becoming a great
coaling station for steamers going to India, China, and
Japan, also for the P. and O. steamers that go to
Australia. I saw five large steamers in at one time
for that purpose.

The heat was greater at Colombo than it had been
at Calcutta, but there was always a fresh breeze blowing
from the sea during the day, which made it more endur-
able; at night the wind blew from the land to the sea
with unfailing regularity. No one living in this variable
climate of ours could believe it possible to foretell with
such certainty what to-morrow is to bring forth in wind
and weather as you can in these Eastern countries.
During the time we were at Colombo we saw the
same conditions from day to day, and were told that
for weeks together it was the same, changes coming
with perfect regularity.

You may recollect the reference to Ceylon in that
well-known hymn of Bishop Heber's commencing, "From
Greenland's icy mountains." The words I refer to are—

> " What tho' the spicy breezes
>   Blow soft o'er Ceylon's isle,
> Where every prospect pleases,
>   And only man is vile."

It may be interesting to you to know in how much that
verse describes Ceylon as we found it, and I am glad

to say that, except on one point, I can vouch for its truthfulness. As regards its "spicy breezes," Captain Anderson, Commander of the *City of Cambridge*, the steamer we went out in, told me that when he happens to be passing the island after nightfall, he could always feel the delicious odour of its aromatic plants upon the breeze which was then blowing from the land. And I can myself attest that I have felt the sweet fragrance in the air as I drove along the highway amongst the cinnamon gardens. The next line, which says that "every prospect pleases," I can also say is true. And now the only point at issue between me and the worthy Bishop is as to the *vileness* of the inhabitants. I am much inclined to think, however, that Bishop Heber did not in this make special reference to the Cingalese at all, but to mankind in general; for, I am bound to say, that beyond a strong desire to get as many rupees as possible for the nick-nacks they sold you, I could discover no special characteristics in the inhabitants of Ceylon to warrant the application of the epithet *vile*.

Part of the time we were in Ceylon we spent at Kandy, a beautiful inland town amongst the mountains, and about 2,000 feet above the level of the sea. Its situation and surroundings are charming. The air is dry and bracing; in fact, it is the sanitorium of Ceylon, and is resorted to by invalids. The railway journey of about 80 miles passes through much interesting scenery, and at one point the road is cut in the face of the solid rock at a great height above the valley below. Coffee and spices used to be the principal products of Ceylon. Of late years the coffee plant has partially failed, and now the plantations have added rice, cinchona, and cocoa, and

I believe tea also is now grown. There is a tradition in
India that Ceylon is the birthplace of the human race;
but their account of the untoward circumstance that
caused man's fall is somewhat different from ours. The
Bible version relates how Adam partook of the forbidden
fruit from the hand of Eve, and then cast the blame
upon her. But the Indian tradition has it that Adam was
more gallant—that he was so enamoured of his young
wife that he preferred to follow her out into the world,
never to return, rather than remain without her, although
surrounded by the manifold attractions of the Garden of
Eden.

There is nothing in the Bible account that forbids
us localising Paradise in Ceylon; and certainly of all
the lovely spots I have looked on there is probably
none which has a climate so agreeably suitable for the
human race, if their clothing was still to be as Adam's
was—an apron of fig leaves. The wondrous beauty
of the sunsets we saw there are ever to be remembered.
The luxuriant foliage of that tropical clime is beyond
description, such brilliancy of colouring everywhere is
nowhere else to be seen. Surely it is of it the poet
speaks when he says—

> " He told of the Magnolia, spread
> High as a cloud, high overhead
> The Cypress and her spire
> Of flowers, that with one scarlet gleam,
> Cover a hundred leagues, and seem
> To set the hills on fire."

We had been a fortnight in Ceylon, and were now
done with India. Old things were to pass away: from
this time onwards we were to be amongst the things

which are entirely new. From Colombo we proceeded onwards to the Australasian Colonies by the steamer *Mirzapore*, belonging to the P. and O. Company. She had a full complement of passengers—upwards of 200 in the cabin.

Again we were favoured with good weather, and a comparatively smooth sea all the way. The only thing notable that occurred during the voyage was a water-spout we saw the third day after leaving Colombo. It appeared to be about two or three miles off, and looked like an enormous mushroom, a stem of ten or twelve hundred feet in height, and then spreading out at top in vapour, whilst all around us in every direction the sky had an unsettled look, and heavy rain fell at short intervals. The previous day we had crossed the equator, and broken weather, which is usual there, con-tinued for some time thereafter. But the passengers were not confined to the cabin, for in all these steamers sailing within the tropics there is an awning over the deck extending from stem to stern to protect you from the sun's says, and of course it is equally serviceable in keeping the rain off; we therefore had perfect freedom to be on deck constantly—indeed, there was a piano fixed on the quarter deck, and we had excellent musicians on board, so that all through the voyage there was a con-tinuous concert. I should not omit to mention that during four days, commencing on the third day out, we sailed through a stretch of ocean not less than 1200 miles in extent, over which was a floating frothy-like material of a brownish colour, some of it in lumps as large as a Swedish turnip, and much of it in pieces like a walnut. Part of it was fished up and found

E

to be lava formation, the supposition being that it was
the debris from the great eruptions at Java, which
had occurred some time previously, and it may be
remembered caused the loss of nearly 100,000 lives.
The commander of the steamer held the opinion, however, that it had not come from that quarter, but more
likely was an eruption beneath the sea near the latitude
we were in. The heat increased as we neared the Equator,
and became quite oppressive, particularly so during the
night, when we were below in bed. Some of the passengers felt it so much that they had mattresses brought
on deck and slept there; but we very soon ran out of
that high temperature, and the weather became very
enjoyable.

The voyage from Ceylon to Australia is about three
thousand miles, and occupied twelve days. On Monday
morning, 18th February, we left Colombo, and on the
second Saturday thereafter we came in sight of Cape
Leeuwin, the south-west point of Australia.

What land we saw as we sailed along the coast
looked bleak and barren, with great patches of sand,
and almost destitute of vegetation, no habitations of
any kind being visible.

The weather had during the last few days become
quite cold, and during the night especially every available covering was acceptable.

On Sunday morning early we entered King George's
Sound, and put out the mails at Albany for Western
Australia. It is quite an unimportant place, and the
steamer does not stop long. We cast anchor off the port
at two in the morning, and started again at seven. A
few of the passengers went ashore to see friends, but

only two left the steamer permanently. King George's Sound is an excellent land-locked harbour, and in former times was much resorted to by whalers, when that industry was prosecuted in the Southern Seas. Whales seem to have deserted the Australian coast now, and the little town of Albany, that used to be a busy place, has of late years rather fallen back.

We had been sailing in a southerly direction from Ceylon, and had not observed a great round swell that was meeting us, coming from the Southern Ocean. When we came out from King George's Sound our course was changed to due east, and so we had this swell on our broadside, which caused the steamer to roll heavily. I recollect immediately when we rounded upon our course after leaving the Sound that the vessel gave a tremendous pitch and roll, dashing the breakfast dishes, that had just been set, into the lee of the cabin floor with a crash that left hardly one whole dish. I do not know who was to blame, but certainly the guards should have been on the tables before coming out. I daresay I heard that the stewards expected we would not sail that morning till after breakfast. In connection with that untoward incident, I was informed that the crockery bill of the P. and O. Company amounts to £10,000 annually.

Our next stopping place was Glenelg, the port for the city of Adelaide, and we reached it on the following Thursday morning. Nearly all the passengers landed, and went up by train to Adelaide, which is seven miles inland. We did so, and breakfasted there, spending the day seeing what was interesting in and around the city. It is a fine city, and is the seat of Government of

South Australia. Parliament and the Supreme Law Courts are there. There are many splendid buildings in it, the larger number, however, are only two storeys in height, but the streets are much wider than in any town I know of the same size at home. This is a favourable peculiarity of the colonies. With the exception of Sydney, all the cities and towns have very wide and regular streets. Generally, too, ample pleasure grounds are provided, and other means of relaxation and enjoyment. It has a free library of 20,000 volumes, and a reference library of 2,000 standard works; but the citizens were not content with these, and I found them expending £95,000 in the erection of a new public library, with art gallery and museum combined, which have since been opened. The former governors, in handing over 23,000 volumes to the new library, said— "The Institute, now supplanted, has done good work in its day, and has been instrumental in scattering the seeds of intellectual cultivation and development far and wide over the colony." Adelaide has a Botanical Garden, beautifully laid out and well kept. They have also started a Zoological Garden, but had only a very few animals when we were there. It seemed to be pretty busy, a good many people walking and driving about. Shops just like those at home, but instead of the canvas sunblinds that our shopkeepers use in summer nearly all had permanent awnings in the main streets, forming a covered way extending to the margin of the pavement, and supported on pillars there.

The population of Adelaide was 45,000 at the last census, but, taking in the suburbs that immediately surround it, there is a population of nearly 100,000. I really cannot tell, however, whether there is any particular trade or manufacture carried on. There did not appear to be. It had more the look of a residential town, resembling Edinburgh in that respect more than Glasgow. I observed that fruit was very good and plentiful, and very cheap. We bought, at threepence per lb., as fine grapes as those raised in the hot-house at home, although a little smaller in size; apples and pears, 1d. and 2d. per lb., both excellent; fine peaches, a halfpenny a piece; and other fruit in like proportion.

It was very cold when we left the steamer, before seven in the morning, but we were advised to make provision for a hot day. We therefore put on our light Indian costume, and it was well that we did so, for before noon the heat was oppressive. When we were in the Botanical Gardens I spoke to one of the keepers, remarking that it was surely unusually hot to-day. He said—"No, the temperature is only 92 degrees in the shade, all last week it was over 100." I expressed surprise at that, but he assured me that it was so, and that he thought Adelaide was the warmest place in South Australia. That last statement I was quite willing to believe, for, as we drove about the city and passed the streets running north and south, the wind that was blowing through them came upon us as if out of an oven. Probably it was the rapid change from the cool temperature we had on board the steamer that made it so uncomfortable, but we all agreed in thinking that the heat and sun that day in Adelaide was more unbearable than what we had experienced in India.

It was the second week in March, which corresponds

to September with us. All along the Australian coast, however, the temperature is much affected by the direction of the wind; if it blows from the north, as it did that day, it will have come over the land and imbibed the heat from it; if from the south, it will have come over the sea, and a few days sailing in that direction would bring you amongst icebergs. The changes from extreme heat to intense cold are therefore sudden, and must be very trying on weak constitutions.

The streets and roads are not kept in the same good condition that we generally have them at home, and that remark applies to America as well as the Colonies. But that is not to be wondered at; it is a very costly thing to make a good street, and it would be very burdensome upon a young community, and all the more from the greater width they generally make them. They do the next best thing, however; they usually introduce tramways earlier than we do in this country. In some towns every second or third street has a line running through it. The condition of the streets for driving over is therefore of less importance when you have so many facilities with the tram-cars. The fares are about the same as in this country. In the Colonies, threepence for the whole distance or any part is the usual charge, and you will sometimes get a ride of more than three miles for that. In the United States it was usually five cents., equal to twopence-halfpenny of our money; and four or five miles was quite a customary journey in the large towns. Of course very few passengers travel the whole distance, but great use is made of the tramways, and it is a cheap and easy way of seeing a town, as carriage hiring is generally dearer than with us, and the roads and streets most uncomfortable to travel over.

In Adelaide we had no friends to visit, and we did not think it worth our while remaining a fortnight till the next steamer came to take us on to Melbourne. No doubt we could have gone overland, but it is said to be a most fatiguing and uninteresting journey. There is only as yet railway part of the way, and the remainder by stage-coach over rough roads. It takes longer to go by land than by sea, and very few choose the land route. On the following Saturday we arrived at Melbourne, our entire voyage taking 20 days, the distance from Colombo to Melbourne being close on five thousand miles.

Not many of the passengers left the steamer for good at Adelaide. Some who did were tourists like ourselves, and it was curious to find them turning up at other places afterwards. We parted with some there whom we had travelled with from Calcutta, and we met them again in Melbourne, Sydney, and Auckland in New Zealand. One Glasgow gentleman, who was in the *Mirzapore* when we joined her at Colombo, left here. He called for us at our hotel in Melbourne when we were absent. We saw his luggage in the hotel we stayed at in Sydney when he was absent in Queensland, and we came together two months afterwards in Auckland. He went with us to the Hot Lake district, called the Wonderland of New Zealand, and we parted with him last at San Francisco. Two young ladies and their brother, who had sailed with us from Calcutta, and stayed at the same hotel with us at Colombo, went by China and Japan. We met again in Washington, United States, and sailed over together in the *Oregon* from New York.

Melbourne is not on the seaboard, but is situated about nine miles up from Port Phillip, upon the river Yarra; or, as I believe it was called by the natives, Yarra-Yarra, which, I understand, signifies "running, running." Port Phillip, at first called Hobson Bay, is quite an inland sea, with a very narrow entrance, through which the tide rushes with great force, making it at times almost impassable except to powerful steamers. We were told that in certain states of the wind it was at the entrance highly dangerous. No doubt that would be when the tide was running out, and a strong wind and large waves from the Southern Ocean were meeting it at the narrow passage which is called "the rip," and is only about a mile broad. The rise and fall every twelve hours of so large a sheet of water as Port Phillip contains must make a great commotion running in and out, particularly so as the passage is not clear all the way across, but is blocked with a reef of rocks extending out nearly a third of its width. No vessel ever enters without a pilot. Port Phillip is, I think, as nearly as possible forty miles square, but it is not deep water throughout; there are some shoals. The channel for vessels of a large size is round the eastern margin; smaller ones can make a straight course in sailing out. The largest vessels do not go up to Melbourne, but discharge and take in cargo at the mouth of the Yarra, at William's Town. The authorities, however, are most desirous to have all the shipping brought up to the city, and are now busy widening and deepening the river. They are also engaged in cutting a passage at a bend, which will shorten the distance by about two miles. It will then be seven miles by river, but to measure in a straight line from the city to the bay is less than five miles; and I met many in Melbourne who held the opinion that it would have been a wise expenditure of public money to have made a cut direct to the bay. The ground was entirely level, and no engineering difficulties seemed to be in the way.   There is a railway from the wharf where the large steamers are berthed ; the carriages come alongside, and passengers and baggage are carried to the city in thirty minutes, where you have to pass the Customs.   The Customs officials were more particular at Melbourne than at Calcutta or Colombo.   Indeed, at Calcutta our baggage was not examined at all, and at Colombo only one box was opened, the officer mentioning that it was done to enable him to say that he had examined it.   At Melbourne our baggage was all opened, but very superficially inspected.   I observed, however, that returned colonists had theirs more carefully looked at, they being much more likely than tourists to bring contraband goods with them.

Our first impressions of Melbourne were most favourable.   It came into view as we sailed towards the wharf at William's Town, and appeared to be a much larger city than we had anticipated.   Spreading in all directions it seemed to cover a great space of ground, and even from that distance we could observe numerous church spires and prominent buildings.   One in particular, with a handsome dome, which we afterwards found to be the International Exhibition building, bore a singular resemblance to St. Paul's Cathedral.   Indeed, in many respects Melbourne brought up the recollection of London more than any other city I have ever seen. Of course it is much less as regards population, but

F

with its surrounding suburbs covers a great extent of
ground. Its original founders were wise in their genera-
tion, and laid off wide streets at regular intervals, thus
preserving good air-channels throughout the city. I
found also that the Legislature had an Amendment of
the Health Act in hand, in which building regulations
had a prominent place. And I may say, not a moment
too soon, for I observed in the very centre of the
business part of the city, narrow passages, which no
doubt had originally been intended only for meuse lanes
to the houses fronting the wide streets; and these were
now being rapidly filled up with buildings. These lanes,
named after the streets they run parallel to, are now called
Little Collins Street, Little Bourke Street, and Little
Lonsdale Street.

There was one other matter, now about to be re-
medied, but which still I must not omit to mention, lest
it should be thought that it had escaped my observation,
or that I approved of the arrangement. I refer to the
open gutters which convey the city sewage to the river.
Even in the principal streets these conduits carry their
filthy load past the noses of the pavement pedestrians,
and in hot weather must be very offensive. When heavy
rains occur the gutters are almost impassable. Indeed,
provision is made for crossing opposite every other shop
door by an arched bridge, 10 or 12 feet long, extending
from the pavement to the street. The River Yarra above
the city is beautiful, but from the city to the sea it is
not attractive; its insanitary condition will soon demand
attention. When thus venturing to criticise the arrangements of Melbourne, we should not forget that the
building regulations of Glasgow are still very defective,

and that we have not yet found any better method of sewage disposal than the objectionable one of pouring it into the Clyde; and so, instead of condemning them, we should rather wonder that towns which have grown so rapidly possess already so many of the comforts and luxuries of city life.

Building ground in the centre of the city brings a very high price. I cannot contrast it with the price paid in Glasgow, where it is sold at so much a square yard. In Melbourne it is sold by the foot frontage. I heard some startling statements of the great advance that had taken place in the value of ground within quite a limited period. Indeed, it is not yet fifty years since the first house was built. One story occurs to me:—A servant girl, some forty years ago, asked her master to put her savings of twenty pounds in safe keeping. He was then purchasing an allotment in Elizabeth Street for a client, and by adding five pounds to the girl's twenty, he bought an adjoining lot for her. That same piece of ground is now yielding a thousand pounds annually. Rents, I believe, are quite as high in Melbourne as in Glasgow.

The International Exhibition Building belongs to the Colony, and has cost upwards of two hundred and fifty thousand pounds. It is a magnificent structure, and being on the highest ground in the city, it is well seen from a great distance all around. In its general form it bears some resemblance to a cathedral, with nave and transept, and a dome rising from the centre.

The length of the building from east to west inside the doorways is 500 feet. A balcony runs round the main building inside, and there are picture galleries east and west thirty feet wide. The walls are of stone,

The dome itself is a massive and elegant piece of work, two hundred and fifty feet in height to the flagstaff that surmounts it. Around the base of the dome, at about two hundred feet from the ground, there is a promenade, from which a magnificent view of Melbourne and the surrounding suburbs can be obtained. There is a large open space around it laid out in pleasure ground, and being near the centre of the city, it is much resorted to, and, along with the building, is used in the same manner as our Crystal Palace at Sydenham.

There is no city that I know of so well off in the matter of pleasure grounds. In and around the city there are eight public parks, and all beautifully kept. The most attractive, however, is the Botanical Gardens, picturesquely situated on the banks of the Yarra. In them are to be found rare shrubs and flowers from every clime. These grounds are very exquisitely laid out, diversified with hill and dale, wood and water, and are open at all times to the public. Government House, the residence of the Governor, is immediately adjoining these beautiful gardens, and its amenity is greatly enhanced thereby. I had the honour of an interview with the Governor, Earl Normanby, to whom I had an introduction from Earl Derby, Secretary for the Colonies.

It is almost impossible to realize that not more than 40 years ago that part near the centre of the city, on which the Exhibition Building now stands, was all covered with the Australian bush, and that lawless freebooters had as secure shelter there as in old times Sherwood Forest afforded to Robin Hood. Now all around for many miles is entirely cleared and the ground laid out in streets and largely built over with terraces and crescents like those of our own west-end.

With the advantages of these extensive pleasure grounds, the people of Melbourne have besides numerous facilities for getting to the country beyond. There is a complete system of cheap omnibuses, and small waggonettes, at the same fares as the omnibuses, plying constantly to the near suburbs. Drivers of these conveyances have much higher wages than those in similar situations at home, but their duties are somewhat extended.

There are no guards upon the omnibuses in the Colonies or in the United States. Passengers are requested to put their fare through a slit in a glass box at the back of the driver's seat, access to which is had from the inside of the omnibus, and when any one requires change, it is got from the driver by passing it through a round hole at his side. When you put your fare through the slit, it remains in sight till he touches a spring, which lets it fall into the box below. No passenger can enter or leave the 'bus without the driver knowing, as he has the door under control by a strap at his hand. If the passenger does not at once put his fare into the box the driver rings a bell. The entrance door is constructed to cover the back steps, and so no one can ride there.

They are now about to introduce tramways, and I was informed that the reason why they had not done so long since was that the company and the corporation could not agree upon the terms. The latter proposed to construct them on a similar footing to ours in Glasgow—which the company, I believe, have at last agreed to; and I understand that since we were there a loan for a large amount has been floated in London to pay for their construction, the City Corporation guaranteeing the payment. Probably the very considerable elevation in the streets leading to the north has been an obstacle to the use of tramways in them. I hope they may have the good sense, when laying down the rails, to make arrangements for working the cars by cable rather than by horses.

The method is very simple. I saw the cable cars running at Dunedin, in New Zealand; at San Francisco, in California; and at Chicago. If you suppose for a moment that the method of pulling the cars is the same as the N.B. Railway have for drawing their carriages up the tunnel to Cowlairs, but that instead of the rope which there runs over grooved wheels above ground, the whole thing — rope and wheels — is placed in a a small tunnel beneath the space between the rails that the cars run on. A longitudinal opening of about an inch wide is made over the top of the sunk tunnel just over the rope, and a strong iron rod fixed to the front of the car passes down through this slit or opening of the tunnel, and by means of a clutch like a pair of nippers seizes on the rope, and thus the car is drawn along. When the driver wishes to stop the car, he does so by letting the nippers open, which lets the rope free, and using the break the car is stopped. By this means a whole city can be worked in the safest and quietest possible manner, and I believe much more economically than by any other way, especially so if there are steep gradients. I am glad to know that there is some prospect of this method being adopted in Edinburgh, and equally sorry that the Corporation of Glasgow have not taken it in the extension of their tramway system now in contemplation, for which the cable cars would have been admirably suited.

The Australians are a sport-loving people.

Horse-racing was going on when we arrived at Melbourne. It was the last of three days' racing, and we had the opportunity of witnessing it. I was the only one of my party who had ever been at any meeting of the kind before, so we accompanied our friends to the course. I must say that if the pastime is to be defended at all the Victorians present the best case possible. It was computed that more than fifty thousand people were present that day; and looked upon from the elevation of the Grand Stand they had a most respectable and orderly appearance. On the Stand itself, which is a handsome permanent building, seated in ascending rows for several thousands, so that every one can see all that is going on in front, the best people of Melbourne were pointed out to us. No public betting is permitted there, the betting men are relegated to an enclosure near the stables, so that anything that might be offensive is in a manner hid.

When the Melbourne Cup is run for it is said that usually eighty thousand people are present. The scene on that day is reported to be unique and imposing. Visitors come from all parts of the country, and in considerable numbers from the adjacent colonies. The city seems to empty itself, as endless lines of carriages, and a vast tide of human beings, hurry to the course by road and rail. A galaxy of wealth, fashion, and beauty appears upon the Grand Stand such as cannot be found elsewhere in the colonies, and which is scarcely outrivalled in Europe.

Horse-racing is probably the amusement that attracts all classes most, but boating, yachting, bowling, bicycling, cricket, lawn tennis, gymnastics, and other recreative amusements have all their share of popularity.

Hotel accommodation in the colonies is as yet rather defective. I do not know whether the circumstance that hotels are so numerous there has anything to do with that, but it is the case that they are to be counted by the hundred; in fact, there are upwards of a thousand in Melbourne, and none of them are very large. No license is granted to any merely wine and spirit shop; all must have the capacity, less or more, of hotels. I was told that no new license is given to any premises now with less than 20 bedrooms, but the license is not withdrawn from smaller houses previously licensed unless for some default. I suppose the object aimed at in only licensing hotels was to discredit dram-drinking. I fear, however, that the invariable bar attached to all of them has somewhat frustrated that desirable object. One effect has been gained, I should think, viz., to quicken the ingenuity of hotel-keepers in finding names to distinguish them. I think it would have been impossible to get a thousand different acceptable names for the Melbourne hotels. I had the curiosity to turn up their Directory at the word Hotel, and, as might be expected I found there were a good many duplicates, and some names were in still higher favour. The Colonists are intensely loyal—no one can now have any doubt of that— and so the prefix Royal distinguishes no less than 42 hotels; Victoria and Queen are also favourites, for 31 have either of these; 26 have Prince or Princess; and a dozen are pleased to be known as British or Britain. I observed that two hotels held out the tempting offer of rest and refreshment beneath the Glasgow Arms. When speaking of these hotels, I should not omit to mention that there were ten under the banner of temperance—three coffee palaces, two of which were the finest and largest I have seen anywhere; they are the property of Joint Stock Companies, and I was told were doing well. The hotel we went to—The Grand—was only opened the week before our arrival. It is one of the largest in the city. We were very comfortable in it, the food was excellent, the attendance good, and all in charge most civil and obliging. The charges we thought very moderate in all the hotels we were in, varying from 10s. to 12s. 6d. a day each for board and lodging, and the same for a private parlour.

You are charged by the day in the Australian hotels, and, indeed, in almost every other country except in Britain. I very much prefer it. Sometimes you may be a gainer by having the several items only charged, if you happen to be absent from many meals; but take it all round, it is much more convenient and simple. I found on board the steamer we went out in many of the Australian gentlemen fretting at the hotel charges in this country, particularly at the item "attendance." "Why," they asked, "should hotel-keepers charge for that which shopkeepers do not? you get attendance from them as well, and it is never specially charged. Besides, the servants in Britain always looked for a tip, notwithstanding paying it in the bill." They hoped that travellers from this side would not introduce the tipping system, they did not like it, but paid their servants well so that it was not looked for. I rather fear that some of the

G

servants have a different opinion on the matter, although
I must admit that they did not show it in any obtrusive
manner.

I should make one exception in regard to hotel charges,
and that was in respect of European wines—which, however, I never heard asked for except on one occasion.
Almost invariably it was the native wine that was drank
at table. Indeed, the price put upon all European wines
was quite prohibitive. I happen to have the Grand Hotel
wine list by me, and I see from it that Burgundy is 20s. a
bottle, Champagnes, 12s. and 13s., Port from 7s. 6d. to 20s.,
Hock from 10s. to 20s., Sherry 7s. 6d. to 12s., and Clarets
5s. to 10s. The highest price for Australian wine on their
card is 4s. for one particular brand, all the others 3s. a
bottle, and I recollect of seeing some of these in grocers'
shops ticketed 1s. a bottle. There is not much wine drank
at the hotel dinner table, but more in the Colonies than
in America, although less there than in this country in
similar circumstances. I observed, however, that some
who took none at the table resorted to the bar immediately
after dinner, and I suspect had something stronger than
wine there. That remark applies to both the Colonies
and America. In both, tea has largely taken the place
of wine at the dinner table.

There appeared to me to be much less drinking
amongst the working-classes in the Colonies and in
America than there is at home. Where the labouring
classes have many opportunities for enjoying themselves
in the open air, they do not so readily resort
to the public-house. The bright, clear atmosphere
so constantly prevailing in Australia and New Zealand
begets no craving for stimulants, as I fear the dull,

depressing climate of this country does. Of course all
the greater merit to those here who withstand it ; but
I feel that allowance should be made for these differing
conditions in which the same classes are placed here
and abroad when we contrast them. There is another
reason for greater sobriety there than here that should
not be overlooked—the working-classes are much better
housed than at home. I question if there is such
a thing as a single-apartment occupancy in Melbourne, while we know there are very many in Scotland,
and particularly in Glasgow. The English style of
cottage building prevails throughout the Colonies, thereby
securing greater privacy and more accommodation. No
doubt it involves higher rents, but then the working
classes have better wages, and can well afford to pay more
rent. The style of living, in short, is altogether above
that of the average of working men in this country, both
as regards food and lodging. But notwithstanding that, I
could not but suppose that there would be some poor
people in Melbourne, as there is in every large city, and
I asked a young friend in the medical profession there to
direct me where to find them. He said—" You had better
get some one to accompany you, as it is best to go at
night, and you would not be safe alone. Saturday
night is the right time, and if you can meet me at ten,
I will arrange to have a detective officer accompany us."
The last Saturday night I was in Melbourne we met
by appointment, and, accompanied by two experienced
officers, inspected the slums in Little Bourke Street, one
of the narrow lanes, and within not more than a stone's
throw of the most fashionable and highly-rented shops
in the city. We plunged into a labyrinth of dark pas-

sages and inferior property that those who only frequent the front streets would never think existed. Some of the houses we entered were Chinese gaming shops, these in many instances crowded to the door, the greatest excitement prevailing amongst the men surrounding the gaming tables, who were all Chinese. The games were quite novel to me; I had never seen the like before, the cards used having Chinese characters, and not the marks that we are familiar with. Our two detectives pushed the bystanders aside to make an opening for us to see the game, which went on all the same. Those in charge knew the detectives well, as they periodically visit, but seldom require to interfere. In some of the houses opium smoking was going on. Those indulging in that were lying on couches and some on beds, but none undressed. The atmosphere in these houses was abominable, such as only a Chinaman can stand. After being in a number of them I explained to the detectives that my young friend had evidently misapprehended my desire and object in the visits we had been making—that it was not the Chinese, but the very poor of the city, I was desirous to see. To my great surprise they informed me that of that class there really was none to take me to. There was an institution, they said, supported by subscriptions, to which the few aged and wholly destitute could go who had no relations to assist them; but of the wretched poor as a class there really was none in Melbourne; and I am bound to say I saw none neither in appearance nor in the act of begging all the four months we were in the Colonies.

The Chinese have the reputation of being clever workers in wood, and I believe many of those in Melbourne are employed as carpenters and joiners. They are also largely engaged in washing and dressing, the laundries being almost entirely in their hands; but probably the employment in which the largest number are engaged is market gardening; in that they greatly excel. I may say, however, that they are not regarded with favour by other workmen, as they are contented with lower wages. There is an agitation on foot in the Colonies to have a capitation tax imposed upon them, as in America.

The recognised working day for artizans and labourers is eight hours. They usually commence work at eight, taking breakfast before that; they go to dinner from twelve to one, and stop altogether at five. I don't think the Saturday half-holiday, that our working-classes lay so much store by, is in practice there. If it is anywhere, it will be got by shortening the meal time, as the full forty-eight hours is held to be the working week.

The figure eight is a favourite one with the working man in Australia. He holds that work should never be prolonged past eight hours a day, that wages should never be below 8s. a day, and that eight hours should be allowed for rest, and eight for play; and from all that I could learn he has fairly well attained to that ideal. Annually there is a great demonstration in honour of the eight-hours movement in Melbourne. It occurred whilst we were there, and took the form of a monster procession such as we had in Glasgow when laying the foundation-stone of our New Municipal Buildings in George Square. Every trade was represented; the various handicrafts were shown in operation, as with us, on platforms erected on large lorries, with flags and banners flying, and with numerous bands of music. It was a gay and imposing scene; but not more so than the magnificent spectacle I had witnessed in our own city just six months before on the occasion I have referred to.

It may be interesting to some to know the wages earned by workers in Victoria. I believe the rates I quote are quite reliable, and they are confirmed in an article in the *Scottish Review* of October last referring to the sister Colony of New South Wales, and I believe may be held applicable to the whole of Australia. Ploughmen receive from 18s. to 22s. 6d. a week; shepherds from £30 to £50 per annum; stock-keepers from £40 to £55; all these having rations added. Masons, carpenters, bricklayers, plasterers, and slaters 10s. a day; plumbers, coachbuilders, brassfinishers, coppersmiths, and the iron trade generally, from £2 5s. to £3 12s. per week; painters and glaziers, 9s. a day; saddlers from 25s. to £2 15s. per week; tanners and curriers from £2 to £3 10s.; tailors from £2 to £3; drapers, salesmen, and upholsterers from £2 10s. to £4; jewellers from £2 15s. to £3 15s.; watchmakers from £3 10s. to £5; lithographers and binders from £2 10s. to £3; compositors, 1s. per 1,000 ens; gardeners from 15s. to 25s. per week; labourers from 5s. to 7s. a day; grooms from 30s. to 40s. a week; coachmen from 35s. to 50s.; married couple, without family, for home stations, from £60 to £90 per annum, with board and lodgings; married couples, with family, from £40 to £50; men cooks on farms and stations, from £45 to £55; female cooks, the same; general servants, nursemaids, and housemaids, from £25 to £35 per annum; milliners from 35s. to £3 10s. per week; needlewomen and dressmakers from 15s. to. 20s.; and tailoresses from 20s. to 35s.

I cannot speak with the same assurance of the remun-
eration available to those in situations where payment is
by salary. I rather fear there are not so many vacancies
to fill as amongst the wage-earning class; and certainly
in no case need any idle, dissolute, or aimless youth go
there—for such there is no opening whatever. Even the
most energetic will likely have difficulties to encounter,
and therefore I would not have any one implicitly
depend that immediately on landing in Australia they
will at once drop into a satisfactory situation. Throughout the Colonies at the present time trade and commerce
are depressed, and many are out of employment. The
authorities, at several of the places we visited, were
providing labour for the unemployed. Besides, it
must ever be borne in mind that the man who can only
turn his hand to one thing is ill-fitted to be a Colonist.
He may, of course, by chance as it were, get the very
thing that suits him ; but it is much more likely that
he may find it necessary to accept any employment
that turns up, and unless he is prepared to do so he
had better stay at home. I heard numerous instances
of prosperous and successful men who had commenced
their careers in the Colonies in quite different callings
from those which they had followed at home. I feel
much responsibility in offering any opinion on this subject. But I am sure I am safe in saying this, that the
man who will get on best in Australia is the active,
industrious fellow who usually gets on well at home.
But, in any case, I would have no one harbour the thought
that in going to the Colonies he is required to make sacri-
fice of the usual amenities of social life, for with confidence
I give the assurance that in the large towns at least he

will find what should satisfy him in all respects. Take
Melbourne, for instance.   It has four daily and two
evening newspapers, with eight additional published every
Saturday—three of which are illustrated.   There are also
several fortnightly and monthly magazines.   To say that
their newspapers are ably conducted is the simple truth,
and it is not too much to say that some of them may well
take rank with the best of our home press, and are far ahead
of the average American newspaper.   In their columns
every morning you will find all the important events of
the previous day recorded that have occurred throughout the world, and extracts from leading British newspapers, all transmitted by telegraph cable.

Amusements of every kind—an Opera House, several
theatres and music halls—an Athenæum and many other
Halls for public meetings.   All the literature that we
possess you will find on the shelves of their libraries and
free reading room.   In the matter of a Free Public
Library Melbourne has set Glasgow a noble example,
for it has provided a splendid building, costing upwards
of a hundred thousand pounds, in which there is sitting
accommodation for 600 readers, and has more than a
hundred thousand volumes in it.   There is also a Picture
Gallery and a Statue Gallery, in which are many rare
works of art; a Museum also, in which there are more
than forty thousand specimens, all labelled and classified.
Churches of every denomination ; and there being no
church established by law the State knows no one
denomination more than another.   The most perfect
religious liberty and equality prevails.   Primary education is entirely free, but under control of the Government ; and promising pupils may win State exhibitions

to carry them to the University and to higher education
in certain special schools and colleges, and therefore I would say that to the man who has only a limited
capital, but who is actuated by an honourable ambition to
get on in the world, and improve the circumstances and pros-
pects of his family, who is not afraid of a little roughness
at first, or of hard toil thereafter, and who can suit
himself to new conditions and take advantage of
them, our own Colonies—Australia, New Zealand, Canada
—present fields of enterprise and usefulness probably
equal to any to be found in the world; and the working
man, when he finds employment there, will have these
advantages over his chances at home—his hours of
labour will be shorter, and the climate being more
genial, he will have greater comfort in outdoor work,
and more opportunities of outdoor enjoyments. His
wages generally will be higher, and his food upon the
whole cheaper. His expenses for dress need not be
appreciably greater; and if he has a family the school-
master will cost him nothing, as education is free to all.
And, finally, if he succeeds in rising above the condition of a wage-earner into that of an employer of labour,
there will likely be a larger number around him who have
travelled the same road to riches as himself than he would
find in like circumstances in the old country.

Whilst speaking thus favourably of life in the Colonies,
I am offering no positive opinion as to the desirability
of emigrating. Everyone must make up his own mind
as to that. It is also of momentous importance to make
the right choice where to go. Various considerations
will influence the decision. All that I desire to say
upon it is, that there is not the slightest necessity for

H

anyone changing his nationality when he leaves these
shores.   Under no other flag that I know of is there
greater freedom; under no other is there a surer prospect
of prosperty, of health and happiness, of true liberty—
civil and religious—than is to be found in that Greater
Britain whose value and importance to us we are only
now beginning to apprehend.   And the only merit which
I attach to the words I am now speaking is, just in so
far as they may influence those who do intend to emi-
grate, not to change their allegiance when they leave us,
but to keep under the old flag, thus remaining still an
integral part of the grand old British Empire.

I need hardly assure you that there is ample space
unoccupied both in Australasia and in Canada; for whilst
in these British Isles there are nearly 300 persons for
every square mile of land, there is as yet only an average
of one person to each square mile on those vast ter-
ritories of which I have been speaking.   A glance at
the map which is now before you will show clearly how
large a country Australia is, and how small in compari-
son to it is Great Britain and Ireland.   But probably
your eyes may not convey to your mind the exact proportion, and you may be better able to form an estimate
when I tell you that Australia is more than 24 times
the size of Great Britain and Ireland, including also the
Isle of Man and the Channel Islands.

I have already said that our first look of Melbourne
brought back the recollection of London to us; and when
you take the population which each of these cities has
within their own municipal bounds, the resemblance is
greater than is generally thought, for both cities, taken in
that way, have just about seventy thousand inhabitants.

Neither city, however, has its population so computed, for London, the capital of England, is acknowledged to contain more than four millions of people, and Melbourne, the capital of Victoria, is put down as having 304,410. This of course, like London, includes its suburbs, and takes in a dozen townships, all having separate government; indeed, there are five of these entitled to be called independent cities—known as the City of Colingwood, City of Fitzroy, City of Richmond, City of South Melbourne, and City of Prahran. Each of these has upwards of 20,000 inhabitants; but I understand that in the colonies the qualification for the title of "City" rests in having a clear public revenue from rates and taxes of £20,000 per annum. That accounts for the city of Melbourne appearing so very extensive, these separate towns being close to it. Indeed, it would not be easy to say, unless with a map before you, where the one ends and the other begins. Melbourne itself, although, as I tell you, containing less than 70,000 of population, occupies an area little short of Glasgow, for it is spread over 5,020 acres, while Glasgow within its Parliamentary boundaries has only 5,063 acres, and on that comparatively small surface there is a population of upwards of 520,000. The entire municipality of Glasgow, however, is 6,111 acres, there having been 1,048 added to it for municipal purposes since the Parliamentary boundaries were fixed in 1832; but on this additional acreage there are only about 23,000 of population. Glasgow, if computed in the same way as London and Melbourne, would be a large city, if the population of its suburbs were included, as they certainly ought to be.

The population of the whole of Australasia is a little over

three millions, and Victoria has nearly a third of the whole;
New South Wales comes next with a population of about
870,000 ; then New Zealand with about the same population as Glasgow, viz., 550,000. The importance of the
Australian Colonies, however, is not to be measured by
the extent of their population, but by the amount of their
trade and also by their prospective future development.
It is a startling and surprising fact that the commerce of
Australia is now greater than was that of the United
Kingdom at the accession of Queen Victoria. The statis-
tics of the Australian Colonies show last year an import
and export trade of one hundred millions sterling, while
that of the United Kingdom in 1836 was only ninety-three
millions.

I felt curious to know how much of this trade came to
Great Britain, and I find that last year we imported from
Australia merchandise to the value of £26,839,490 sterling,
and we exported to them £25,936,201. The trade of
Australia therefore with the mother country in 1883 has
been nearly fifty-three millions sterling.

Victoria, which in wealth and population has hitherto
been regarded as the most important of the Australian
Colonies, imposes the highest import duties on manu-
factured goods ; in point of fact, it may be said
to have a protective tariff, and raises a large portion
of its revenue by duties on imported articles, the
professed object being to encourage home manufactures.
New South Wales and the other colonies impose somewhat
lower duties, and may be considered in a measure free.
The colonies have great emulation, and are very jealous of
each other. Victoria is now being hard pressed for the
foremost place by its sister colony ; in fact, in the matter

of foreign trade, New South Wales has now gone ahead of Victoria, for its imports in 1883 were three millions, and its exports three and a half millions sterling greater, whilst upwards of a million more tons of shipping visited the free trade colony.

Of course none of them is absolutely free. They have all less or more import duties, the difference being in degree. Victoria puts high duties upon such goods as can be made in the colony, with a view to keeping the home trade to itself, and employing its own people. They thus in a measure loose the stimulus of foreign competition. The other Colonies exact lower duties, and for public revenue only, just as Britain does. We profess to be a free trade country, but we are only so to a certain degree, for in 1883 we levied customs duties on upwards of thirty millions sterling of imported goods, seven millions sterling of which were from our own Colonies; seventy thousands pounds' worth came from Australia. The goods from Australia on which import duty is levied, I presume, would be wine. I do not know of any other commodity that Australia produces on which duty would be exigible. Tobacco is grown in some parts, but I am not aware that it is exported to this country.

As regards the Australian wine, I believe it has greatly improved of late years. The earlier exportations did not give satisfaction. The colonists seemed to think that a poor and cheap wine would compete most successfully with the vintages of Europe. But such quality did not keep well, becoming sour and otherwise getting out of condition, thus bringing discredit on the production. They are now, however, giving greater attention to this branch of industry, and producing a really good wine, which I understand is finding favour in this country and in America.

We were about two months in Melbourne (we made it our headquarters), but in the course of that time we visited Sydney, the capital of the adjoining colony, and made excursions to other towns and places of interest in the interior.

I had been hearing of some wonderful trees that could be seen not very far away from Melbourne, and on inquiring at a friend I found they could be reached in one day's journey by road and rail. Accompanied by my friend, my son and I made an early start by railway to Lilydale ; breakfasted there, and proceeded onwards by 4-horse coach to Fernshaw, where we lunched. Whilst waiting till the horses were brought out I got into conversation with the landlord, asking him if we were far from the big trees. He said that we were just about to ascend the Black Spur — a mountain covered with a dense forest extending over many miles, and there I would see them. I spoke incredulously of the great height they were said to be. He felt a little offended, and said to me, "If you come to my back garden you will see one that fell there a year ago, and you can measure it yourself. It is not by any means one of the largest, but I daresay *you* have never seen one so large." I went with him and saw the immense tree. It had fallen across the river, and I passed over it, and walked along the trunk up into the wood beyond —its length being 381 feet. We started on foot ahead of the coach, and had walked several miles up the Black Spur before it overtook us, and so had ample opportunity of examining the giants of the forest. Never before had I seen such tall trees, and probably never will again, unless I return to Australia. For although the trees in California have more timber than these, they do not grow so high. Many of those we were looking on were upwards of 400 feet, and we were informed that some 500 feet in height were to be found. These great trees are of the Eucalyptus tribe, a species of gum tree, of which there are 27 varieties. Those we saw were perfectly straight and carry no branches on the first 150 or 200 feet of their length, and I would say were 50 to 60 feet in circumference.

It was about 70 miles to Marysville, 40 miles of the distance over such roads as we never see in this country ; and some portion of the journey was over what is called "Corduroy," which simply means cut trees laid across the road, and you can understand the shaking which travelling over such as that involved. Another country trip we took was to Fern Tree Gully, a well known resort of excursionists, about 20 miles from Melbourne. The forest scenery there is splendid, and abounds with tree ferns 30 and 40 feet in height and beautifully furnished. It is noteworthy to relate that at a small place which I went to see named Sorento, some 30 miles from Melbourne—a place as yet in its infancy, for there were not more than 200 of resident population—I observed a solitary, although rather an imposing building in the middle of a sandy waste; it was a mechanics' institute, furnished with a free library of 500 volumes, erected by the proprietor of the estate as an attraction to working men. I suspect in this country we are more accustomed to seeing property owners planting spirit shops at the corners of their streets to attract large rents into their own pockets.

We visited Sydney also, the capital of New South Wales. We went to it by sea and returned by railway. The great feature of Sydney is its splendid natural harbour. We would not call it a harbour at all, any more than we call the Frith of Clyde one from the Cumbraes upwards; and the harbour of Sydney is even more extensive than all that. I have heard it said that the shore-line surrounding it measuring up the numerous indents and around the various bays would count up a total of over 1,100 miles. I had not the curiosity to test the calculation by exploration or otherwise, but I could well see that the shore-line was very great indeed. The city is almost completely surrounded by water, and presents most admirable facilities for carrying on its great and rapidly increasing maritime trade. Perhaps no port in the world has a larger fleet of small passenger steamers than Sydney has plying to the various landing places surrounding its capacious harbour. I recollect asking one of the captains of the little craft if he knew how many there were. He replied there must be three or four hundred. He returned to me before I left his steamer and said he had understated the number by fully a hundred. I expressed surprise, but he assured me he was correct, and, pointing into a bay we were then passing, he asked me to count how many were there. I made out 18, but he showed me there were five more; in fact, you can form no conception of their number from anything of the kind to be seen elsewhere.

The fare charged is generally very moderate, and they seemed to get plenty to do. It was the Easter holidays when we were there, and both horse racing and boat racing were in full swing. Hanlan, the celebrated Canadian sculler, was there, and had received an ovation on his arrival such as we in this country reserve for distinguished generals or eminent statesmen. Donald Dinnie, the Scottish Athlete, was drawing crowds to see his feats performed when we were in Melbourne, and I have no doubt would be welcomed heartily when he went to Sydney.

There are splendid building sites for villas and mansions well taken up all along the opposite shores fronting the harbour, but the city itself did not impress us so favourably as Melbourne had done. There was an hour's rain just before we landed—the first that had been for many weeks. The streets were in a sad condition with mud. I never before had seen anything so bad, although I cannot say that now—for I have seen worse since in America, yet it is the fact that they were almost impassable. Fortunately, however, for our subsequent comfort, there was one entire night's extremely heavy rain, and the next day (Sunday) the city presented quite a changed appearance of cleanness. The streets generally are much narrower than those in Melbourne, but numerous fine buildings — both public and private—are in them ; indeed, I believe a greater number of beautiful structures are to be found in the one city than in the other, but very many of them are in a measure lost to observation from their position. The Town Hall, or, as we would call it, the Municipal Buildings, is of great size, with a tower 200 feet high, and from a balcony near the top a magnificent view is got all over the harbour and its surroundings. It is quite an ornament, in the very centre of the city. The Post Office also is an imposing edifice of beautiful construction, with a collonade of grey granite pillars around it. The Museum and Picture Gallery also, and Free Library, with 50,000 volumes on its shelves, are handsome structures. The streets of Sydney are better paved than those of Melbourne, and quite recently the Corporation have determined to spend a further sum of two hundred thousand pounds in wood paving, which, from the nature of the climate, I expect will stand well there. At present, also, the city is engaged in a gigantic sanitary scheme, whereby the sewage which now pollutes their harbour will be carried to the sea coast, some six or seven miles away. I called repeatedly at the City Surveyor's office to learn the particulars of the undertaking, but it was the Easter holidays and I did not succeed in finding him. I had the opportunity, however, of inspecting the works, which consist mainly of tunnelling through rock at a considerable depth, and must cost a large sum to execute.

Sydney was originally a penal settlement. It was to this point on the Australian coast that the first settlers came 100 years ago, after leaving Botany Bay, where they originally landed, but which they soon found to be unsuitable on account of deficient water supply. We were curious to see the place where Captain Cook had set up the British flag and took possession of Australia for Britain ; one of the branches of the steam tramways leads to it. He named it Botany Bay because of the great quantity of rare plants which a botanist who accompanied him collected. Our opinion was, that he had collected them too carefully, and left none remaining, for it appeared to be the most desolate and barren spot we had seen all around the city. For nearly 50 years Sydney remained the only port of any consequence in Australia. All home and foreign business was transacted there, but its rapid rise to a great commercial centre was not foreseen, and no proper care seems to have been taken in forming the streets upon a regular plan. Perhaps the configuration of the ground on which it is built is partly the cause. The city is situated upon a peninsula of about a mile and a half in length by half a mile in breadth, and being nearly surrounded by deep water, its facilities as a maritime port are of the first order. It has extensive wharfs and warehouses, and a complete system of steam tramways connecting it with populous suburbs. Ample railway accommodation also, which maintains its intercourse with the country beyond, and extending to the border-line of the adjoining colony of Victoria. By an unfortunate difference in the gauge of the state railways of Victoria and New South Wales, the whole traffic is blocked at the boundary, and both goods and passengers have to be transferred from the carriages on the narrow gauge of the one system to those on the broader gauge of the other. The distance by rail between the two capitals is 574 miles, and the time occupied in travelling is nineteen hours, the fare 81s. first-class, and ten shillings additional for sleeping berth. The journey is by no means an interesting one, as much of the way is through partially cleared forest, the blackened tree stumps and burned bush presenting rather a dreary aspect. One railway journey we took from Sydney to the Blue Mountains was more attractive—it brought back the recollection of the Himalaya railway to Darjeeling—

for here again we were climbing the steep mountain by aid of the iron horse. Part of the way up the gradient is very great—being 1 in 30, and that portion of the line is called the zig-zag, by reason of its tortuous turnings, threading its way amongst peaks and crags to the mountain top, from whence the view is splendid. The zig-zag is considered a marvel of engineering skill, the line at parts being on the very brink of a precipice. It is said that 5 miles of this portion cost over one hundred thousand pounds a mile to make; the fifty miles of the Darjeeling railway cost only one hundred and fifty thousand altogether; but this railway has been of much service in opening up the country beyond. We spent 10 days in and around Sydney. It is a thriving city, and appears to be carrying on an extensive trade. If Melbourne could be likened to London, with as much truth might Sydney be spoken of as resembling Liverpool.

After returning to Melbourne, we went from thence to Geelong, a seaport town on Port Philip Bay, about 40 miles from Melbourne, and holding communication with it by steamboats and railway. Geelong is rather a slow place, there being very little stir about it. There are some large mills manufacturing woollen goods, and a few ships come to load grain, but the town had rather a dull look, after having been in Sydney and Melbourne. But Geelong, with a population of only ten thousand, has a mechanics' institute and a free library, with fifteen thousand volumes. From it we went to Ballarat, some sixty miles inland, and where at one time much gold was found. The whole of the ground for miles around has been carefully searched, and had the appearance of wrought-out brickfields. Now, the gold is only found at a considerable depth beneath the surface, embedded in quartz, which, when brought up, is crushed under powerful machinery, and the particles of gold washed out. There was one nugget found here that sold for £10,500. Ballarat — this town in the midst of the Australian gold fields—has a mechanics' institute and a free library, with twenty-five thousand volumes. Its population is forty thousand, and largely composed of miners, who seemed to be a quiet, industrious, and orderly people. From Ballarat we went to Sandhurst, a whole day's journey further inland, and it, too, is a great seat of the gold mining industry; it has a population of 30,000. It also has its mechanics' institute and free library, with ten thousand volumes, besides an institution called a School of Mines, with all necessary appliances for giving working men instruction in their leading industry. In early days Sandhurst, then called Bendigo, was a prolific gold field, and numerous large finds of gold were made, near the surface, in its neighbourhood. Now, however, what is called alluvial searching is all over, and gold is only found at considerable depths. Two of my party accompanied me to the underground workings of the South St. Mungo Mine, a hundred fathoms deep, where the miners had just come upon a valuable seam of quartz that promised large dividends to its shareholders. We were taken to it by a gentleman who had gone to Sandhurst from Glasgow 35 years ago. Not a single house was then erected, the entire plain was covered with tents, and many scenes of disorder occurred before any settled government was instituted. His occupation was that of provision dealer; and it was most interesting to hear from him the adventures and almost insurmountable difficulties of bringing goods up from Melbourne in bullock waggons, a distance of over 100 miles, there being no other road than a rough track through the bush, taking sometimes a month to traverse. Contrasting that with the well-appointed railway which now connects the two cities showed no greater change than from the canvas town of 30 years ago to the handsome city buildings that are now in Sandhurst. Our old Glasgow citizen is now a retired man, the possessor of much property. He has occupied the Mayor's chair with satisfaction to his fellow-citizens, and is still a member of their Town Council. He told me he had returned to the old country a few years ago, after 25 years' absence, intending to settle down here for the rest of his life. Seven months of a Scottish climate was all that he could endure. Our changeable gloomy weather was too severe a contrast to the almost continuous sunshine of Australia, and so he went back again to spend his last years in the new country of his adoption. I met not a few who had a similar experience to relate; and very many who said, "We would like to see the old Country once more; but to stay there permanently, no, that's not good enough."

It was principally to meet friends in Melbourne that our visit to the Colonies was made, otherwise we no doubt would have taken the shorter route round the world, and gone by China and Japan; but we were amply rewarded in going to the Colonies, not only by the great pleasure of meeting those whom we had been parted from for more than thirty years, but also in seeing the marvellous progress which these young communities are making.

Often before I went there had I wondered why our friends did not return to this country again. I cannot now say that I am surprised at all. In even less time than 30 years old ties are partly broken, and new ones formed where you live. You have got used to a climate so different from that prevailing here—which you now feel would be unbearable, and there then remains nothing but the sentimental attachment to the country that gave you birth; but how strong that attachment is amongst the Colonists I had many opportunities of witnessing. I shall never forget the delightful surprise I got the first Saturday night I was in Melbourne. We went to an entertainment in the City Hall, at which three or four thousand people were present. At the conclusion of the concert the great organ—said to be the fifth largest in the world—pealed forth the "National Anthem," and the whole audience rose at once to their feet. I thought then I had never heard the familiar air sound so gloriously. In no other four months of my life have I heard it more frequently than during those four months I spent in the Colonies. I confess to you that nothing I heard or saw when out there was so pleasing and surprising as the intense feeling of loyalty manifested everywhere—even the very children, who were never out of Australia, speak to you with a delighted expectancy of some day going "Home."

www.ingramcontent.com/pod-product-compliance
Lightning Source LLC
Chambersburg PA
CBHW030011030726
47499CB00008B/3002